W9-ATT-516

CRYSTAL LAKE PUBLIC LIBRARY
3 2306 00531 2700

Under the Sea

Sea Urchins

by Jody Sullivan Rake

Consulting Editor: Gail Saunders-Smith, PhD

Consultant: Debbie Nuzzolo
Education Manager
SeaWorld, San Diego, California

Mankato, Minnesota

Pebble Plus is published by Capstone Press,
151 Good Counsel Drive, P.O. Box 669, Mankato, Minnesota 56002.
www.capstonepress.com

Printed in the United States of America

1 2 3 4 5 6 12 11 10 09 08 07

Library of Congress Cataloging-in-Publication Data
Rake, Jody Sullivan.
Sea urchins / by Jody Sullivan Rake.
p. cm.—(Pebble Plus. Under the sea)
Summary: "Simple text and photographs present the lives of sea urchins"—Provided by publisher.
Includes bibliographical references and index.
ISBN-13: 978-0-7368-6724-5 (hardcover)
ISBN-10: 0-7368-6724-4 (hardcover)
1. Sea urchins—Juvenile literature. I. Title.
QL384.E2R25 2007
593.9'5—dc22 2006013648

Editorial Credits
Mari Schuh, editor; Juliette Peters, set designer; Kim Brown, book designer; Wanda Winch, photo researcher/photo editor

Photo Credits
Jeff Rotman, 1, 5, 13, 15
Seapics.com/Andrew J. Martinez, 16–17; James D. Watt, 6–7, 20–21
Tom Stack & Associates Inc./David Fleetham, 8–9; Tom Stack, 18–19; Tom & Therisa Stack, cover
Visuals Unlimited/Ken Lucas, 10-11

Note to Parents and Teachers

The Under the Sea set supports national science standards related to the diversity and unity of life. This book describes and illustrates sea urchins. The images support early readers in understanding the text. The repetition of words and phrases helps early readers learn new words. This book also introduces early readers to subject-specific vocabulary words, which are defined in the Glossary section. Early readers may need assistance to read some words and to use the Table of Contents, Glossary, Read More, Internet Sites, and Index sections of the book.

Table of Contents

What Are Sea Urchins?

Sea urchins are
ocean animals.
They look like
little round porcupines.

Most sea urchins are
about the size of a tomato.
Some are as big
as a grapefruit.

Body Parts

Sea urchins have hard shells
covered with spines.
Spines keep sea urchins
safe from predators.

Sea urchins have mouths
on their bottoms.
They have five teeth
that grind food.

mouth

Sea urchins use
their strong tube feet
to walk along
the ocean floor.

What Sea Urchins Do

Sea urchins move slowly.
Their feet grab rocks
to move forward.

Sea urchins search for food on the ocean floor. They eat algae and mussels.

Some sea urchins
burrow into rocks
to hide from predators.

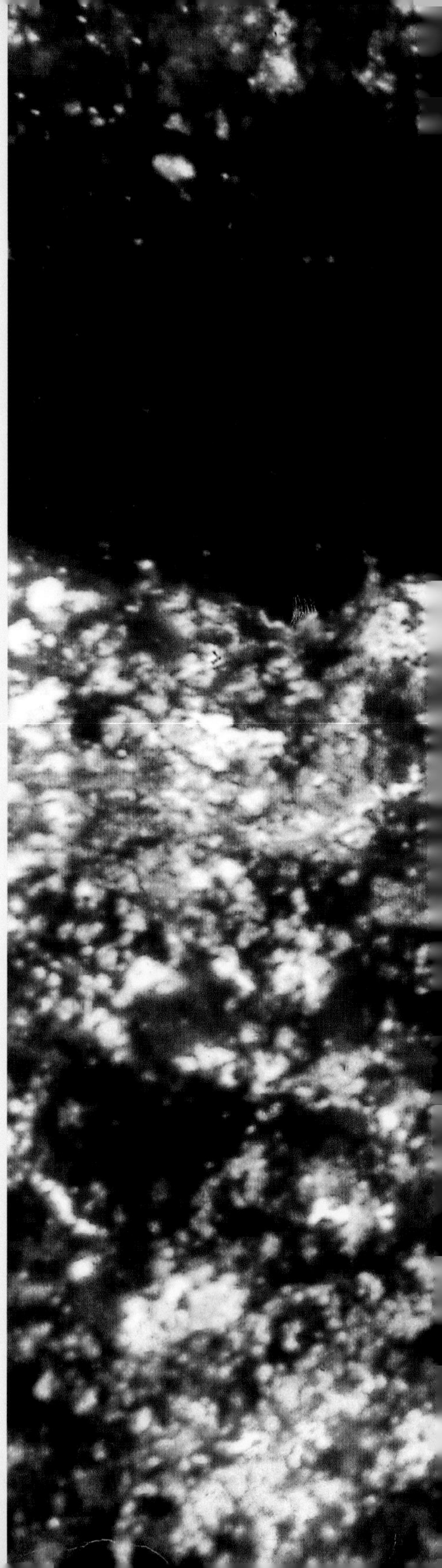

Under the Sea

Sea urchins
make their homes
under the sea.

Glossary

algae—plants without roots or stems that grow in water; sea urchins eat algae.

burrow—to dig a tunnel or hole

grind—to crush or wear down

mussel—a type of shellfish with two joined shells

predator—an animal that hunts other animals for food

spine—a sharp, stiff, pointed part of a plant or animal; a sea urchin's spines protect it from predators.

tube—a hollow cylinder that is open at both ends; a sea urchin's feet are shaped like tubes.

Read More

Gilpin, Daniel. *Starfish, Urchins, & Other Echinoderms.* Minneapolis: Compass Point Books, 2006.

Klingel, Cynthia, and Robert B. Noyed. *Oceans: A Level Two Reader.* Wonder Books. Chanhassen, Minn.: Child's World, 2002.

Schaefer, Lola M. *Sea Urchins.* Heinemann Read and Learn. Chicago: Heinemann, 2004.

Internet Sites

FactHound offers a safe, fun way to find Internet sites related to this book. All of the sites on FactHound have been researched by our staff.

Here's how:

1. Visit *www.facthound.com*
2. Choose your grade level.
3. Type in this book ID **0736867244** for age-appropriate sites. You may also browse subjects by clicking on letters, or by clicking on pictures and words.
4. Click on the **Fetch It** button.

FactHound will fetch the best sites for you!

Index

Word Count: 113
Grade: 1
Early-Intervention Level: 14